TREASURE ISLAND

by ROBERT LOUIS STEVENSON

#4 Pirate Attack

Adapted by Catherine Nichols

Illustrated by Sally Wern Comport

Sterling Publishing Co., Inc.
New York

Library of Congress Cataloging-in-Publication Data Available

10 9 8 7 6 5 4 3 2 1

Published by Sterling Publishing Co., Inc.
387 Park Avenue South, New York, NY 10016
Copyright © 2007 by Sterling Publishing Co., Inc.
Illustrations © 2007 by Sally Wern Comport
Distributed in Canada by Sterling Publishing
c/o Canadian Manda Group, 165 Dufferin Street
Toronto, Ontario, Canada M6K 3H6
Distributed in the United Kingdom by GMC Distribution Services
Castle Place, 166 High Street, Lewes, East Sussex, England BN7 1XU
Distributed in Australia by Capricorn Link (Australia) Pty. Ltd.
P.O. Box 704, Windsor, NSW 2756, Australia

Printed in China
All rights reserved

Sterling ISBN-13: 978-1-4027-4120-3
    ISBN-10: 1-4027-4120-0

For information about custom editions, special sales, premium and
corporate purchases, please contact Sterling Special Sales
Department at 800-805-5489 or specialsales@sterlingpub.com.

Contents

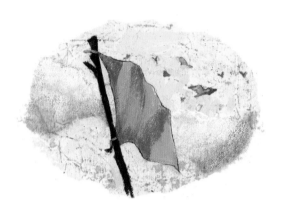

Waving the White Flag

Jim Hawkins was a small boy
on a big adventure.
He had sailed with friends
to Treasure Island.
But pirates were
on the island, too!
The pirates wanted
the treasure buried there.
But first they needed the map
that Jim's friends had.

Luckily, Jim and his friends
found a fort
with a cabin.
It would help
keep them safe
from the pirates.

The morning after
finding the fort,
Jim awakened to the sound of voices.
He was the last one up!
Everyone else was busy working.
Suddenly, Jim heard a cry.
He ran outside.

The ship's captain
had spotted the leader
of the pirates—
Long John Silver!
"He's coming to the fort!"
the captain shouted.

Jim looked
through a hole
in the wall.

Long John was waving
a white flag.
That meant he
wanted to talk,
not fight.

An Offer

The captain let Long John
come inside the fort.
"I have an offer to make,"
said Long John.
"What is it?"
asked the captain.

"I want the treasure map,"
said Long John.
"If you give it to me,
I'll take you to an island
where you will be safe."

Long John held out his hand.
"Is it a deal?" he asked.

"It is not," said the captain.

He did not shake the pirate's hand.

"But I have an offer
for you and the other pirates,"
the captain said. "Give yourselves up.
I will take you home.
You will have a fair trial.
I give you my word."

Long John threw
the white flag
on the sand.
"We will never give up!"
he said. "Soon you'll wish
you had taken my offer."

Jim watched Long John go.
The pirate was angry.
Next time, he would be back
to fight, not talk.

Attacked!

The captain had his men
line up at the wall.
That way they could
see the pirates
if they attacked the fort.

But the pirates were quick.
They rushed at the fort.
They climbed over the wall
like monkeys.

Now the pirates were
inside the fort!
They wanted
the treasure map!
Where was it?

Jim ran
into the fort's cabin.
The map was sticking out
of a jacket pocket.
Jim snatched it and ran.

Outside, there were pirates
everywhere.
One pirate was running
toward Jim!

Jim had no time to be afraid.
He jumped out of the way—
and slipped!

Down the hill Jim rolled!

At the bottom,
Jim got to his feet.
He wasn't hurt,
but where was the map?

Jim looked around.
There it was,
in the tall grass!
He ran over and picked it up.
Jim hid the map
inside a tree.
It would be safe there.
Then he went up the hill
to help his friends.

At the top of the fort
Jim let out a cheer.
"Hooray!" he cried.
The captain and his men
had won the battle.
The pirates were gone.

A Hero

Jim's friends were
inside the cabin.
There was Squire Trelawney,
whose ship they had sailed on,
and David Livesey, a doctor.
Both men were upset.
The captain was trying
to calm them.

"What's wrong?" Jim asked.

"The pirates are gone,

and that is good."

"Yes," said the squire,

"but so is the map!"

"The pirates must have found it,"

said the doctor.

Jim didn't like to see
his friends upset, but he
couldn't stop laughing.
"What's so funny?"
asked the captain.

"I know where
the map is, sir," said Jim.
All three men stared at him.
Jim told them his story.
"So the map is safe," he said.
"I hid it in a tree."

The captain shook Jim's hand.
"That was quick thinking,
young man," he said.
"You are a hero."
Jim felt proud.
The map was safe.
The pirates would not
be back today.
For now, they were safe
on Treasure Island.